MW00487506

DEX T-REX
THE MISCHIEVOUS LITTLE DINOSAUR

WRITTEN, ARTWORK & COVER BY: KATYA BOWSER

STAN LEE - CREATIVE DIRECTOR

PARIS KASIDOKOSTAS LATSIS - PUBLISHER

GILL CHAMPION - EXECUTIVE PRODUCER

TERRY DOUGAS - PUBLISHER & EDITOR IN CHIEF

BILLY PICHÉ - VP OF DEVELOPMENT & PRODUCTION

ALEXIS VAROUXAKIS - VP OF DEVELOPMENT & PRODUCTION

1821 MEDIA - EXECUTIVE PRODUCER

POW! ENTERTAINMENT - EXECUTIVE PRODUCER

Dex T-Rex: The Mischievous Little Dinosaur, July 2014, published by Stan Lee's Kids Universe. 205 S. Beverly Dr. #205 Beverly Hills, CA 90212. Copyright 2014 Stan Lee's Kids Universe. All Rights Reserved. All characters, the distinctive likeness thereof and all related indicia are trademarks of Stan Lee's Kids Universe. ISBN 978-1-939981-02-8. Printed in China. ID: Tracking:

Dex T-Rex loved to play.

On beautiful days,
just like today.

A fun game to play was the
Dinosaur game.

After all, he is a dinosaur,

as stated in his name.

DEX T-REX

He started with the grass

And gave it a big kick,

And broke in half
a poor
little stick.

He roared at the dandelion right in its face,

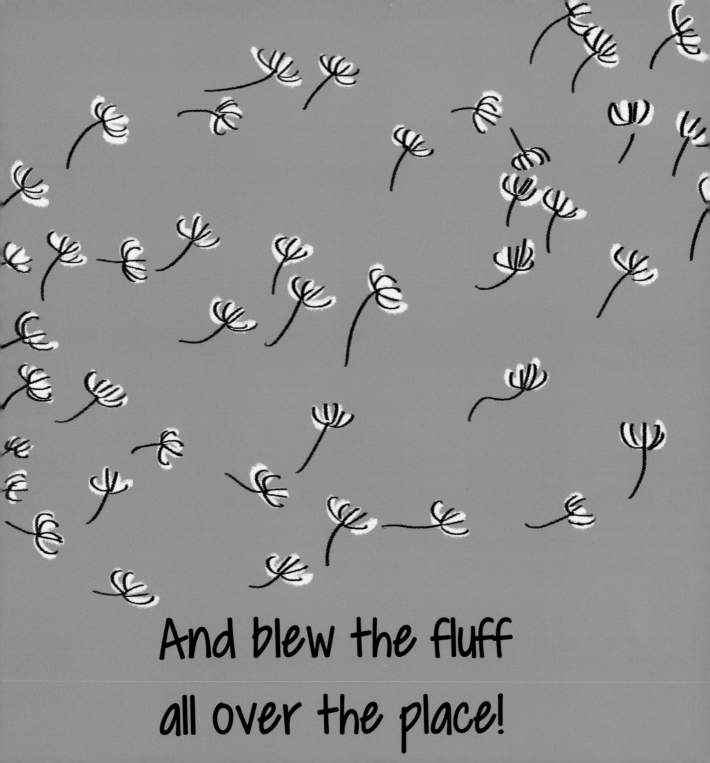

And blew the fluff
all over the place!

He came to a bush

and chewed up its leaves.

And stomped on some flowers

with all too much ease.

He splashed
the water

and chased
every bubble,

Without a care
of getting in trouble.

Then, just for fun,
he butted his head
into a nearby tree

And out fell a caterpillar,
as dazed as it could be.

Dex looked at the caterpillar and felt really sad.

He wished he could undo all the things he did today.

"That's what I'll do!" he told himself with a little smile.

"From now on I'll only do things that are worthwhile."

"I'll tape up the leaves

and fix the flowers with glue."

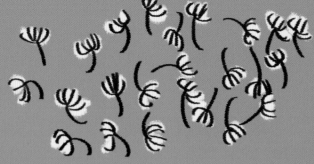

He grabbed all the fluff

and jammed it back in.

He tied up the stick,

and fixed the grass
with a pin.

Then, to the caterpillar, young Dex swore...

Never to harm anything anymore.

THIS EXCITING FOLLOW-UP TO
MONSTERS VS. KITTENS TEACHES KIDS
THAT BEING DIFFERENT IS A GOOD
THING, AND ENCOURAGES THEM TO BE
HAPPY JUST THE WAY THEY ARE.

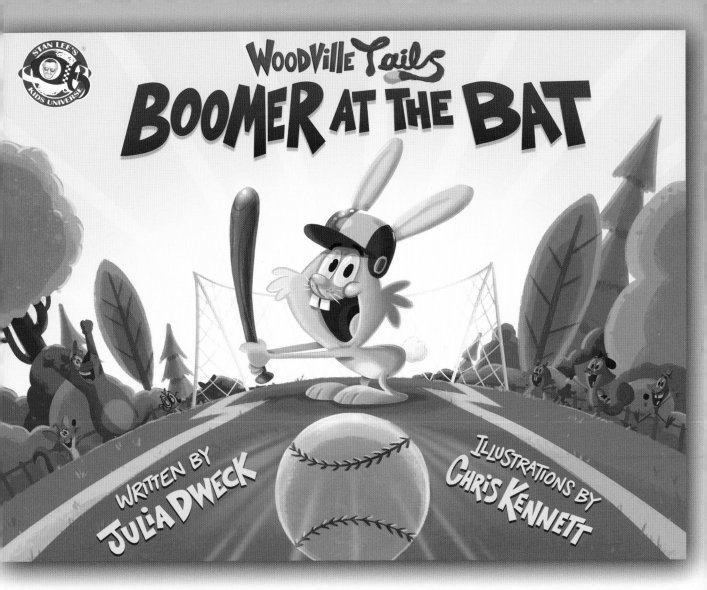

WOODVILLE TAILS
BOOMER AT THE BAT

WRITTEN BY JULIA DWECK

ILLUSTRATIONS BY CHRIS KENNETT

WOODVILLE TAILS: BOOMER AT THE BAT IS FROM BEST-SELLING AUTHOR JULIA DWECK AND ARTIST CHRIS KENNETT. BOOMER THE RABBIT STEPS UP TO THE PLATE AND MUST SCORE A FINAL RUN TO SAVE THE GAME FROM THE CLUTCHES OF DEFEAT. WITH EVERYTHING RESTING ON HIS LITTLE SHOULDERS, WHAT WILL BOOMER DO? THIS FUN BOOK HIGHLIGHTS THE IMPORTANCE OF TEAMWORK AND SPORTSMANSHIP.

ALSO AVAILABLE FROM
STAN LEE'S KIDS UNIVERSE...

www.**StanLeesKidsUniverse**.com

 StanLeesKidsUniverse

 StanLeesKidsU